D1452004

"Satchel" PAIGE

1st ANNUAL
ALL-STAR
GAME
KANSAS CITY MONARCHS
with
SATCHEL PAIGE
— vs —
ALL-STARS
PITTMAN STADIUM
Fayetteville, N. C.

SOUTH'S B...

Satchel Paige
Formerly With Cleveland Indians

J. Armentero...

PITTSBURGH
Craws
FORDS

Advance Tickets 1.00^{Tax}_{Incl.}$ - At Gate 1.25^{Tax}_{Incl.}$
Children 50c
Tickets On Sale At Usual Places

Come
Early For
Choice
Seats

SWINGING FOR THE
FENCES
LIFE IN THE
NEGRO LEAGUES

LEGENDS OF THE LEAGUES

PETE
DIPRIMIO

PURPLE TOAD
PUBLISHING

Printing   1   2   3   4   5   6   7   8   9

PUBLISHER'S NOTE
This series, Swinging for the Fences: Life in the Negro Leagues, covers racism in United States history and how it affected professional baseball. Some of the events told in this series may be disturbing to young readers.

SWINGING FOR THE
FENCES
LIFE IN THE
NEGRO LEAGUES
A 4 VOL. SERIES

A Whole New League
by Wayne L. Wilson
Barnstorming
by Michael DeMocker
Legends of the Leagues
by Pete DiPrimio
Breaking the Barriers
by Russell Roberts

ABOUT THE AUTHOR: Pete DiPrimio is an award-winning sports writer for the *Fort Wayne (Indiana) News-Sentinel,* a long-time freelance writer, and a member of the Indiana Sportswriters and Sports Broadcasters Hall of Fame. He's been an adjunct lecturer for the National Sports Journalism Center at IUPU-Indianapolis and for Indiana University's School of Journalism. He is the author of three nonfiction books pertaining to Indiana University athletics and more than 20 children's books. He has finished one novel and is working on a second.

Publisher's Cataloging-in-Publication Data
DiPrimio, Pete.
   Legends of the Leagues / written by Pete DiPrimio.
      p. cm.
Includes bibliographic references, glossary, and index.
ISBN 9781624692826
1. Negro leagues—History—Juvenile literature. 2. Baseball—United States—History—Juvenile literature. I. Series: Swinging For The Fences : Life in the Negro Leagues.
   GV865.A1 2017
   796.357
Library of Congress Control Number: 2016937176
ebook ISBN: 9781624692833

TICKETS

COOL PAPA BELL

CHAPTER ONE

Cool Papa Bell was in his baseball prime in the 1930s. He was so fast he could out-run truth—but not bigotry. Because he was black, Major League Baseball (MLB) banned him.

Being banned didn't break him. He was made of tougher stuff.

"I don't have any regrets about not playing in the majors," he once said. "They say that I was born too soon. I say the doors were opened too late."

It still made him sad, though. MLB officials would say: "If we find a good black player, we'll sign him." Bell replied, "They was lying."[1]

Cool Papa spent long days in battered buses and motorcars. He and his teammates traveled thousands of bad-road miles from small town to small town across the Midwest. Negro League teams, short on cash, competed against local teams sponsored by steel mills, coal mines, and railroads.

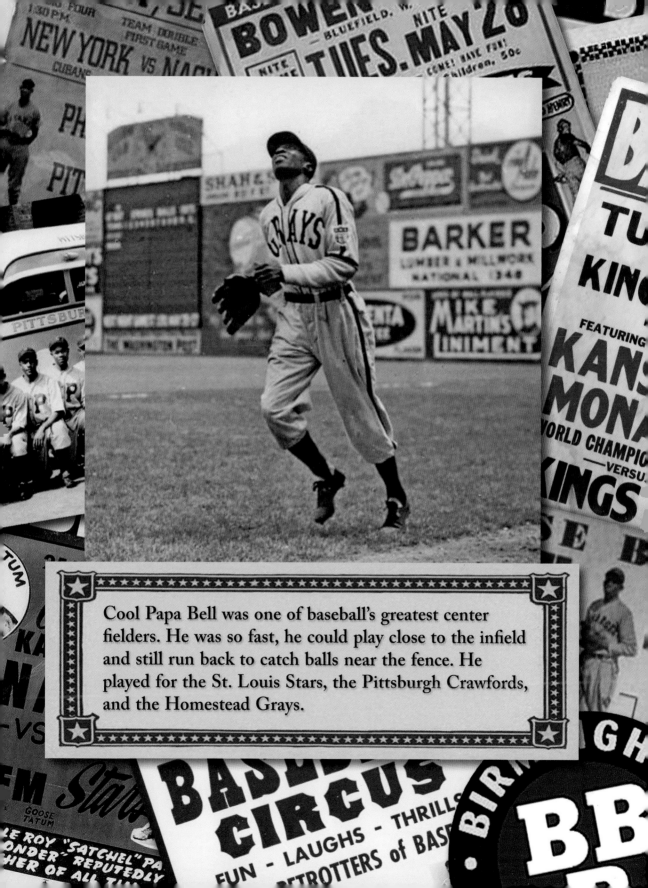

Cool Papa Bell was one of baseball's greatest center fielders. He was so fast, he could play close to the infield and still run back to catch balls near the fence. He played for the St. Louis Stars, the Pittsburgh Crawfords, and the Homestead Grays.

For extra pay, Negro League players would play up to three games a day.

Negro League players would also have exhibitions against MLB players in major league stadiums. Those games often paid better than Negro League games, which didn't draw as many fans. Negro League games drew bigger crowds on Sundays. That was the best day for black fans, many of whom could afford to see only one game a week. To bring in even more spectators, the best pitchers pitched on Sundays.

African-American players played hard, but also with flare and fun—they wanted to make sure fans were never bored. Even their names were fun: Double Duty Radcliffe, King Tut, Possum Poles, Bunny Downs, Rats Henderson, Ready Cash, Spoony Palm, and more.

William Walker "Ready" Cash of the Philadelphia Stars.

Few players were as fun as Cool Papa. His real name was James Thomas Bell. He got his nickname in 1922 as a 19-year-old rookie with the Negro League's St. Louis Stars. He found out he would be pitching against one of the best hitters in the league, future Hall of Famer Oscar Charleston. Cool Papa calmly won a one-run decision. He hit a home run and struck Charleston out. That's when teammates started calling him "Cool." St. Louis manager Bill Gatewood thought that wasn't enough, and suggested "Cool Papa."

Cool Papa Bell played professional baseball for 24 years, but he never made it to the Major Leagues.

The name stuck.

Cool Papa was born in 1903 in Starkville, Mississippi. His parents were sharecroppers (farmers who worked land owned by others), but Cool Papa had no interest in that.

"I just had baseball on my mind," he said.[2]

He left Mississippi for St. Louis when he was 17. He planned to go to night school, but instead played baseball. Two years later he was playing professionally.

When Cool Papa's pitching arm went dead early in his career, he became a switch-hitting center fielder, smacking hits from both sides of home plate.

Cool Papa Bell might have taken more extra bases, like turning a double into a triple, than any player in history. He is shown reaching third base during a 1932 game.

How fast was Cool Papa? Hall of Fame pitcher Satchel Paige once said Cool Papa "hit a line drive right past my ear. I turned around and saw the ball hit him sliding into second."[3]

According to other tall tales, Cool Papa once scored from first on a bunt; he beat out groundballs hit to the pitcher; he stole two bases on one pitch. He reportedly could run all around the bases (360 feet, or 120 yards) in 12 seconds. The most famous story said Cool Papa was so fast, he'd hit the light switch to turn the lights off and was tucked in bed before the room went dark.

According to the Baseball Hall of Fame, Cool Papa hit .316 with 133 stolen bases, but no one really knows. Records were more guesswork than fact in the Negro Leagues. Cool Papa said in one game he had

Cool Papa was so fast, he once scored from first off a bunt.

five hits and stole five bases, but it was never recorded. As he explained it, "They forgot to bring the scorebook to the game that day."[4]

Still, in 1933, he was credited with 175 steals in 200 games.

After his playing days were over, Cool Papa coached the Kansas City Monarchs. He then became a night watchman at St. Louis City Hall. He lived with his wife Clarabelle in an old redbrick apartment building. In 1974, he became the fifth Negro League player inducted into the Hall of Fame. He died in St. Louis in 1991 at the age of 87.

Although he never played in the majors, a statue of him was dedicated at the St. Louis Cardinals Busch Stadium in 2002.

He had outrun bigotry after all.

The Cardinals honored Cool Papa with a statue, even though he never played for them.

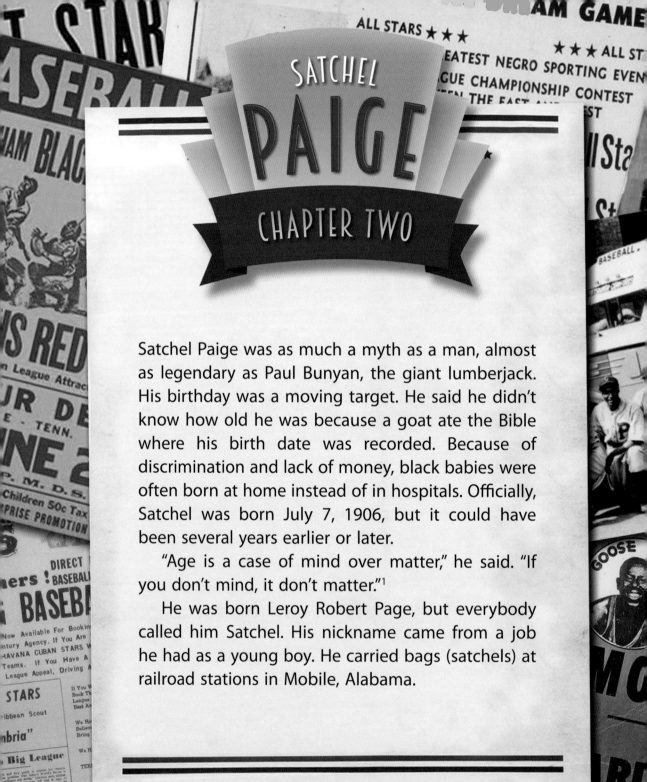

SATCHEL PAIGE

CHAPTER TWO

Satchel Paige was as much a myth as a man, almost as legendary as Paul Bunyan, the giant lumberjack. His birthday was a moving target. He said he didn't know how old he was because a goat ate the Bible where his birth date was recorded. Because of discrimination and lack of money, black babies were often born at home instead of in hospitals. Officially, Satchel was born July 7, 1906, but it could have been several years earlier or later.

"Age is a case of mind over matter," he said. "If you don't mind, it don't matter."[1]

He was born Leroy Robert Page, but everybody called him Satchel. His nickname came from a job he had as a young boy. He carried bags (satchels) at railroad stations in Mobile, Alabama.

Satchel Paige was skinny but mighty. He threw hard when he was young, smart when he was old, and was funny all the time. He was as famous for his sayings as he was for his baseball records.

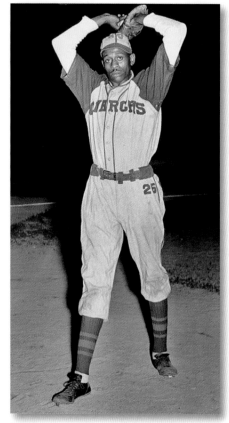

Batters never knew what to expect when Paige went into his windup.

Satchel grew up in Mobile, and along the way his mother added an "i" to the Page name. Satchel said she thought it added quality. He was the seventh of twelve children and sometimes struggled with being good. Starting at age twelve, he spent five years at an Alabama reform school for stealing and for skipping school. The school's baseball coach, Edward Byrd, saw promise in Satchel. He helped him develop into a star. Although skinny (Satchel would joke that if he stood sideways you couldn't see him), he mastered a high-kicking windup that kept batters guessing.

Satchel could pitch and dance and talk. Boy, could he talk. His sayings are also the stuff of legends. Some of them make you think twice: "Ain't no man can avoid being born average, but there ain't no man got to be common." He also said, "I ain't ever had a job. I just always played baseball."

In his prime, Satchel was banned from Major League Baseball because of his skin color. When the rules changed, he was

Paige and his wife, Janet Howard

still good enough to make the majors—at the age of 42. He dominated early with a fastball Hall of Famer Joe DiMaggio called "the best I've ever seen."[2] Later, he won with experience, intelligence, and creativity.

Satchel last played in the major leagues in 1965 when he was—probably—59. That was twelve years after he'd officially retired. In his last game, he threw three shutout innings for the Kansas City Athletics.

Satchel had pitched against major leaguers for a long time. During off-seasons from 1934 to 1945, he competed in exhibition

The 42-year-old MLB rookie made a big impression.

games against Hall of Fame pitchers Dizzy Dean and Bob Feller. These games were played in MLB stadiums such as New York's Yankee Stadium and Pittsburgh's Forbes Field. In one exhibition against Dean, Satchel retired all 18 men he faced, 13 by strikeout. Cleveland Indians owner Bill Veeck called another Satchel-Dean exhibition "the greatest pitchers' battle I have ever seen."[3]

How good was Satchel? He once threw 62 straight scoreless innings. He had a winning streak of 21 games, threw 50 no-hitters, and, in 1933, went 31-4. He once won three games in one day.

Satchel loved to joke and trash talk and showboat. Some considered him a clown. Those who underestimated him learned to regret it. He won 103 games in the Negro Leagues (he might have won more, but he was often used only for the first few innings to draw fans). He won 28 more in the majors, and who-knows-how-many exhibitions and winter league games. He went 6-1 as a 42-year-old MLB rookie for Cleveland in 1948. In 179 big-league games, he never committed an error.

In 1971, Satchel became the first Negro League player inducted into the Hall of Fame. In 2006, a statue of him was installed at Cooper Park in Cooperstown, New York, the site of the Baseball Hall of Fame and Museum. Satchel Paige Elementary School in Kansas City is named for him.

Teams sometimes honored Paige with a rocking chair. He was old by player standards, but he never let age slow him down.

Paige died of a heart attack in Kansas City in 1982 when he was 75 years old. The stories about him, and his sayings, continue to live on: "Work like you don't need the money. Love like you've never been hurt. Dance like nobody's watching."[4]

Satchel's Sayings

Satchel had many famous sayings on many topics. Here are some of them:

"Mother always told me, if you tell a lie, always rehearse it. If it don't sound good to you, it won't sound good to no one else."

"I never rush myself. See, they can't start the game without me."

"If a man can beat you, walk him."

"It's funny what a few no-hitters do for a body."

"One time I snuck a ball on with me and when I went to winding up, I threw one of them balls to first and one to second. I was so smooth I picked off both runners and fanned the batter without that ump or the other team even knowing it."

"I never threw an illegal pitch. The trouble is, once in a while I would toss one that ain't never been seen by this generation."

Satchel also had six rules for staying young:
1. Avoid fried meats, which angry up the blood.
2. If your stomach disputes you, lie down and pacify it with cool thoughts.
3. Keep the juices flowing by jangling around gently as you move.
4. Go very light on the vices, such as carrying on in society. The social ramble ain't restful.
5. Avoid running at all times.
6. Don't look back, something may be gaining on you.[5]

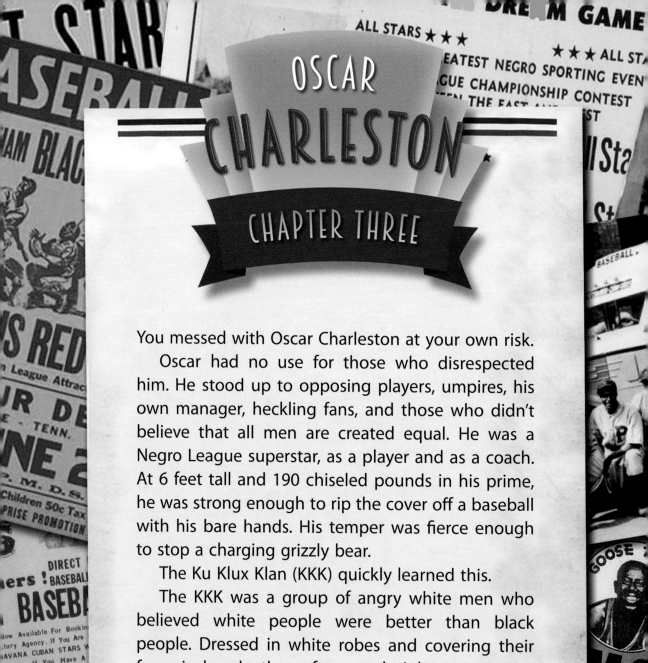

OSCAR CHARLESTON

CHAPTER THREE

You messed with Oscar Charleston at your own risk.

Oscar had no use for those who disrespected him. He stood up to opposing players, umpires, his own manager, heckling fans, and those who didn't believe that all men are created equal. He was a Negro League superstar, as a player and as a coach. At 6 feet tall and 190 chiseled pounds in his prime, he was strong enough to rip the cover off a baseball with his bare hands. His temper was fierce enough to stop a charging grizzly bear.

The Ku Klux Klan (KKK) quickly learned this.

The KKK was a group of angry white men who believed white people were better than black people. Dressed in white robes and covering their faces in hoods, they often used violence to try to get their way.

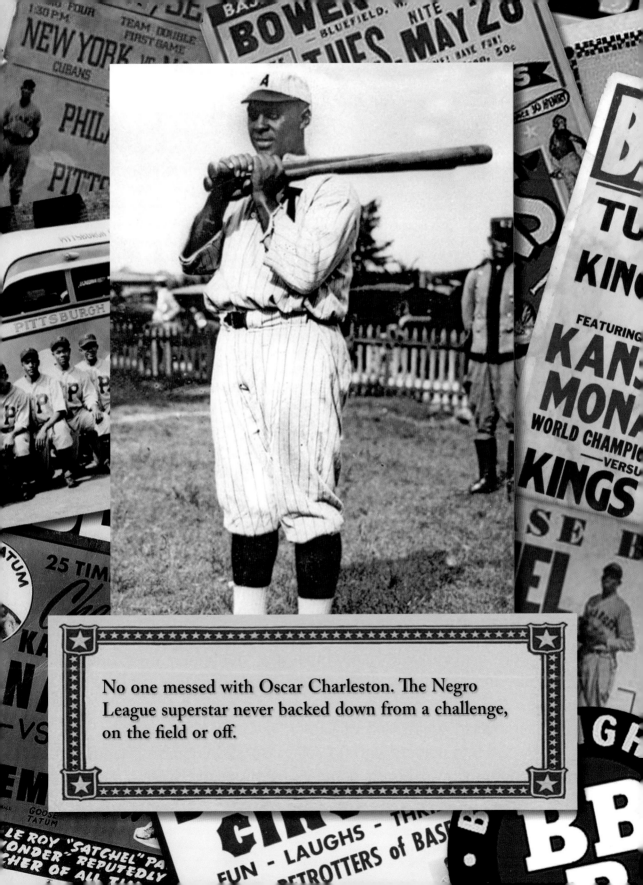

No one messed with Oscar Charleston. The Negro League superstar never backed down from a challenge, on the field or off.

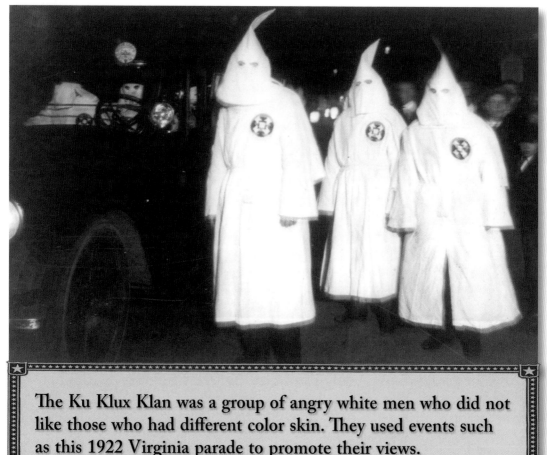

The Ku Klux Klan was a group of angry white men who did not like those who had different color skin. They used events such as this 1922 Virginia parade to promote their views.

After a game in Florida, Oscar and some teammates were leaving the park when a group of KKK men confronted them. Oscar's teammates backed away, but Oscar strode straight to the leader and ripped off his hood. He glared with cold, blue-gray "gunfighter eyes" and told them all—in clear and powerful words—to leave.

They did.[1]

Oscar rivaled white Hall of Famer Ty Cobb for aggressive, nasty play. He slid into fielders with his spikes up, slashing arms, hands, and legs without mercy. "This is a game you're supposed to play, and you're

Ty Cobb's slides often injured other players.

supposed to play it rough, and you ain't got no business complaining," he once said.[2]

No other Negro League player could match Oscar's combination of power, speed, skill, and fearlessness. An Indiana native, he earned the nickname Hoosier Comet. Years after he died, baseball expert Bill James rated Oscar as the fourth-best player of all time, behind only Babe Ruth, Honus Wagner, and Willie Mays.[3]

Oscar was born in Indianapolis in 1896, the seventh of eleven children. He was the son and grandson of construction workers and carpenters, and his love of baseball showed up early. In his early teens, he was the batboy for the ABCs.

Oscar lied about his age so that he could join the army at 15 years old. He served with the 24th Infantry in the Philippines from 1910 to 1915. In 1914 he became the only black baseball player in the Manila (Philippines) League. He also ran track, recording a 23-second 220-yard dash time. That was almost as fast as the winning 1912 Olympic time of 22 seconds.

Oscar became a corporal during World War I. Years later, during World War II, he served at a post in Philadelphia.

After leaving the army in 1915, he returned to Indianapolis. He joined the ABCs, first as a pitcher, then as center fielder. Oscar was a

Oscar Charleston

huge draw. Even his fellow Negro League players were in awe. "You had to see him to believe him," Satchel Paige said.[4]

But his temper often got him in trouble. He attacked an umpire, got into a fight with his manager, and started a brawl with white St. Louis Cardinals pitchers. The Indianapolis ABCs kept him because he was such a great player.

During the 1920s, Oscar played winter ball in Cuba. He became the Cuban League record holder for batting average and stolen bases. (Forty-three years after his death, he would be named to the Cuban Baseball Hall of Fame.)

In 1920, the Negro National League opened for play. In that league, Oscar became a fearless outfielder. He caught any ball that stayed in the park, and sometimes those that didn't. He was famous for leaping over outfield fences to rob hitters of home runs. With one of the

SANTA CLARA B. B. C.

Charleston - Outfielder.

Baseball cards of Negro League stars such as Oscar Charleston are collector's items.

strongest arms professional baseball had ever seen, he could throw runners out from anywhere on the field.

Negro League star Ben Taylor said Oscar was "the greatest outfielder that ever lived—the greatest of all colors. He can cover more ground than any man I have ever seen."[5]

The left-handed batter rocked the Negro Leagues by hitting for average and power. He ran so fast, he sometimes bunted for hits, and often led the league in steals. Although the

Ben Taylor hit .300 or better in 15 of 16 seasons in the Negro Leagues.

records are sketchy, we know Oscar hit better than .400 four times. He had at least a .353 lifetime batting average with nearly 200 home runs. He also hit .326 in exhibition games against MLB teams. He hit .361 over nine seasons in the Cuban League, with a best of .405 in 1922.

In one exhibition series against the St. Louis Cardinals, he hit five home runs in five games. Three times he singled, then he yelled to the pitcher that he was going to

Charleston won championships as a manager and as a player.

Charleston played one season for the Homestead Grays before joining the Pittsburgh Crawfords.

steal second on the next pitch. He did.

He played for 27 years on some of the greatest Negro League teams, including the Homestead Grays and the Pittsburgh Crawfords. He played with, and then managed, many star players. Hall of Famer Josh Gibson was one of them.

In the late 1940s, Oscar scouted the Negro Leagues for Brooklyn Dodgers owner Branch Rickey. He was looking for the right player to break the MLB color barrier. He found him at the University of California—Jackie Robinson. He also helped another black player reach the majors: future Dodgers Hall of Fame catcher Roy Campanella.

Brooklyn Dodgers manager and scout Oscar Charleston

After Robinson, more and more black players were able to play for Major League Baseball. Negro League baseball began to fade. During those years, Oscar managed the Indianapolis Clowns to titles in 1950 and 1954. Shortly after the second championship, when he was 57 years old, Oscar died. He was buried in a small cemetery on Indianapolis' west side.

In 1976, Oscar was inducted into the Hall of Fame. As one Negro League player said, "He wanted to know, was you a crybaby or was you a man. He was that type of manager. He was nice to talk to, he just didn't back down from nobody."[6]

While with the Indianapolis Clowns, Charleston worked with Connie Morgan (right), one of the few women in the Negro Leagues, as well as Richard "King Tut" King.

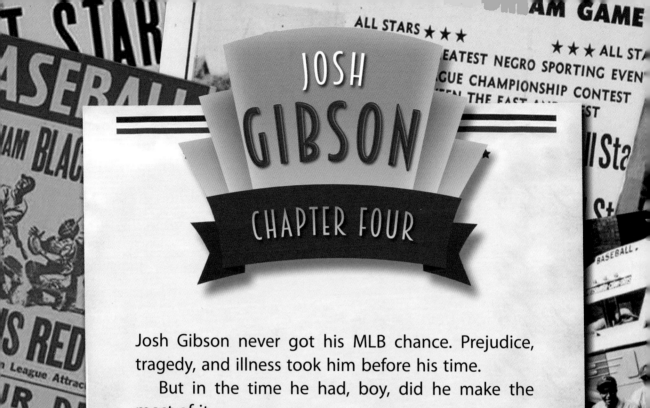

JOSH GIBSON

CHAPTER FOUR

Josh Gibson never got his MLB chance. Prejudice, tragedy, and illness took him before his time.

But in the time he had, boy, did he make the most of it.

In 1998, *The Sporting News* rated him number 18 among its best 100 players of all time.

"I played with Willie Mays and against Hank Aaron," Hall of Famer Monte Irvin said. "They were tremendous players, but they were no Josh Gibson."[1]

Hall of Fame pitcher Satchel Paige played with Josh on the Pittsburgh Crawfords. He said Josh was "the greatest hitter who ever lived. He couldn't have played in those ballparks with the roof on 'em. He would have hit 'em through the roof."[2]

When it came to hitting, Josh was Superman. The 6-foot-1, 215-pound slugging catcher blurred the

Josh Gibson might have been not only the best-hitting catcher of all time, but also the best hitter ever. He was known as the Black Babe Ruth because he didn't just slug home runs, he hit them farther than anybody else.

How powerful was Josh Gibson? He reportedly once hit a home run nearly 600 feet.

line between truth and fantasy. Called the Black Babe Ruth, he hit for average and power. His home runs traveled farther than anyone thought possible. They went farther than those hit by Babe Ruth, Ted Williams, or any other great white slugger.

Josh once hit a home run 575 feet during a game in Monessen, Pennsylvania. In one story, he knocked a speaker off the roof at Comiskey Park in Chicago. In another, he scattered kids out of trees around Washington's Griffith Stadium. The only other player to ever hit it out of Griffith Stadium was Yankees superstar Mickey Mantle.

A 1967 Sporting News article mentioned a Josh homer at New York's Yankee Stadium. It hit a wall 580 feet from home plate. Negro League player Jack Marshall said Gibson once hit a ball out of Yankee Stadium, which had never been done before—although there is no proof to back that up.

Perhaps the best story is about a home run Josh hit at Pittsburgh's Forbes Field. It soared so high, it never came down. The next day, while Josh was at bat in Philadelphia, a ball suddenly fell from the sky

and was caught by an outfielder. The umpire called Josh out—from the previous day in Pittsburgh!

It's been written that Josh hit as many as 84 homers in a season (the MLB record is 73 by Barry Bonds), and once hit as high as .518 for a season (the MLB record since the start of the twentieth century is .427 by Nap Lajoie). His lifetime batting average is .384, although the Hall of Fame has it at .359. His Hall of Fame plaque says he hit almost

Negro League teams sometimes played in major league parks. Josh Gibson scored for the Homestead Grays during a 1940 game at Chicago's Comiskey Park.

Gibson was so good at hitting at a young age that people told stories about him while he was a teenager, before he even joined the Negro Leagues.

800 homers in his 17-year career, and might have hit close to 1,000. He is listed as winning nine home run titles and four batting crowns.

Two MLB teams—the Pittsburgh Pirates and the Washington Senators—wanted to give Josh a tryout in the late 1930s. But because Josh was black, they never did.

One story tells how Pirates owner Bill Benswanger signed Josh to an MLB contract in 1943. Baseball commissioner Kenesaw Mountain Landis tore it up. Another story says Dodgers manager Leo Durocher thought it would be great to have Josh join the Dodgers. Landis penalized him just for saying so.

Racism took away money and fame, but not respect.

Josh, the son of a poor sharecropper, was born in Georgia in 1911. His family moved to Pittsburgh in the 1920s. He started playing

Judy Johnson

semipro baseball and quickly became known for his hitting.

Josh's pro break came when he was 18. He was watching a game between the Homestead Grays and the Kansas City Monarchs when the Grays catcher hurt his hand. Homestead manager Judy Johnson had heard about Josh. He went into the stands to ask Josh if he would catch in the game. Josh said yes, and signed a contract the next day.

That began a career that included stops in Mexico and Puerto Rico. But in 1930, his life took a turn. His 17-year-old wife, Helen, died giving birth to twins, a boy and a girl. He began drinking and doing drugs, but he still managed to play.

In 1943, he started getting bad headaches. In January of 1947, he died

When Gibson stepped to the plate, everybody watched.

As a catcher, Gibson had a strong arm and quick feet. He was almost as good at fielding as he was at hitting.

suddenly of a stroke. He was just 35.

Three months later, Jackie Robinson played his first game with the Brooklyn Dodgers.

A Negro League teammate and friend, Ted Page, believed more than illness killed Josh. He said Josh wanted to be the first to break the color barrier—and Brooklyn Dodgers owner Branch Rickey nearly signed him before Jackie Robinson. However, Rickey thought Robinson would be better able to turn the other cheek when racism flared. The disappointment hurt Josh more than any headache.

"He knew he wasn't going to make the big leagues," Page reportedly said. "They say a man can't die of a broken heart, and I guess that's true. But I tell

you this—all of this lessened Josh's will to keep going and fighting to stay alive."[3]

For nearly 30 years, Josh's body lay in an unmarked grave in a Pittsburgh-area cemetery. In 1975, baseball commissioner Bowie Kuhn and a former Pittsburgh Crawford teammate donated money for a headstone. It reads, "Legendary Baseball Player."

In 1972, the Committee of Negro Baseball voted him into the Hall of Fame.

He had finally made the majors.

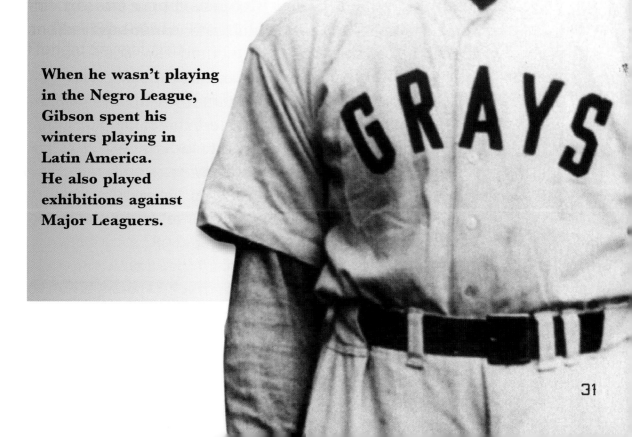

When he wasn't playing in the Negro League, Gibson spent his winters playing in Latin America. He also played exhibitions against Major Leaguers.

31

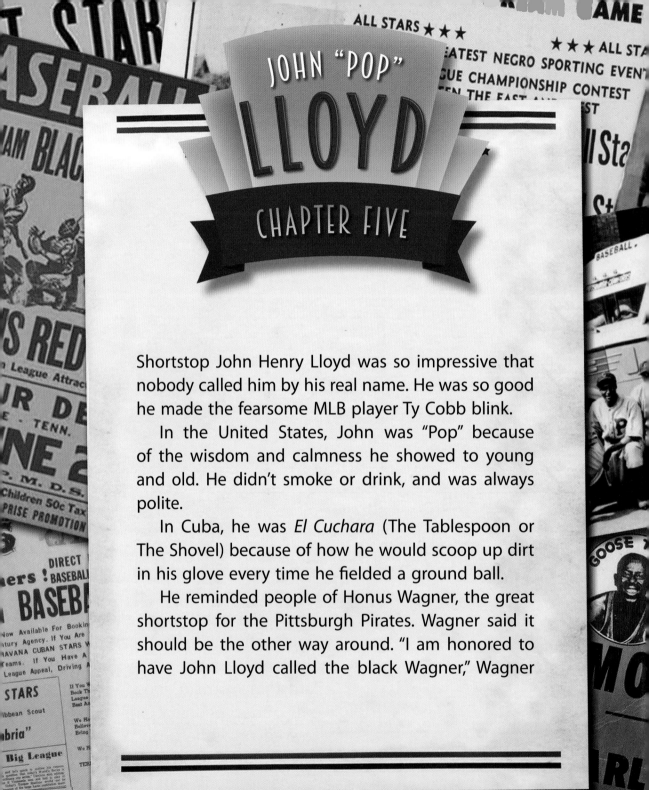

JOHN "POP" LLOYD

CHAPTER FIVE

Shortstop John Henry Lloyd was so impressive that nobody called him by his real name. He was so good he made the fearsome MLB player Ty Cobb blink.

In the United States, John was "Pop" because of the wisdom and calmness he showed to young and old. He didn't smoke or drink, and was always polite.

In Cuba, he was *El Cuchara* (The Tablespoon or The Shovel) because of how he would scoop up dirt in his glove every time he fielded a ground ball.

He reminded people of Honus Wagner, the great shortstop for the Pittsburgh Pirates. Wagner said it should be the other way around. "I am honored to have John Lloyd called the black Wagner," Wagner

John Lloyd was called Pop because he was a gentleman on and off the field. He was also the best shortstop in Negro League history.

Hall of Famer Honus Wagner

once said. "It is a privilege to have been compared to him."[1]

Cobb wasn't as impressed. He was well known for his racist ways. A great hitter with a bad attitude, Cobb wanted nothing to do with black people. In 1910, Cobb and his Detroit Tigers went to Cuba for a five-game exhibition series with the Havana Reds. Pop joined Havana so that he could face Detroit. Lighting up Tigers' pitchers, he went 11-for-22. This .500 average was far better than Cobb's .369.

Cobb was so angry, he vowed never to play against black players again.

Pop's playing in that series impressed John McGraw, the Hall of Fame manager for the New York Giants. McGraw said if Pop were white, "we would show the National League a new phenomenon."[2]

Pop was born in Palatka, Florida, in 1884. His father did not stick around. Pop had to leave school early to help the family by working as a delivery

John McGraw

boy. As a teenager he began playing with a Jacksonville sandlot baseball team. They called him "Just In Time," because he would wait to throw out batters until just before they got to first base, then laugh at them.

He also played catcher for a semipro team in Georgia. The team was so poor, he had to use a wire basket for a catcher's mask.

Harry Buckner, Rube Foster, Sol White, and other black players and managers saw Pop play in 1905. A year later, Pop had signed with the Negro League's X-Giants. He was 5-foot-11, 180 pounds, and could get to almost any ball from his position at shortstop.

Pop helped his teams not just to win, but to win big. Championships were common. In 1913, with Pop playing and managing, the New York Lincoln Giants went 101-6.

1912 New York Lincoln Giants. Top row, left to right: Bill Francis, Pete Booker, John Henry Lloyd, George Wright, Spot Poles. Bottom row: Ashby Dunbar, Louis "Santop" Loftin, Smokey Joe Williams, Hutchings (mascot), Dick Redding, Bill Pettus, Charlie Bradford.

Pop Lloyd

Pop loved to play and live well. He once said, "Wherever the money was, that's where I was."[3] He moved from team to team, often in the same season, depending on who paid more. He played on 12 Negro League teams, and more in Cuba and elsewhere.

Through it all, he kept hitting. In 1928, at the age of 44, he led the Eastern Colored League in hitting (.564) and home runs (11). He played in what was called the "dead-ball era," when baseballs were softer and not as lively as they are now. It was hard to hit home runs, so Pop quickly learned to hit where fielders weren't. When he retired in 1932, he had a career batting average of .343 and 133 stolen bases. These numbers are just a guess, though, because of poor record keeping. They also don't count his 12 winter seasons in Cuba.

Babe Ruth said that Pop was his choice as baseball's best-ever player.

Pop retired from professional baseball in 1932, but not from the sport. He played semipro ball into his 60s. He moved to Atlantic City and became a janitor for the

George Herman "Babe" Ruth

post office and the school system. He also served as commissioner for Atlantic City's Little League. The city named a baseball park for him, the John Henry Lloyd Park, in 1949.

During the dedication ceremony, Pop was asked if he had regrets about never playing in the majors. He answered, "I do not consider that I was born at the wrong time. I felt it was the right time, for I had a chance to prove the ability of our race in this sport . . . and we have given the Negro a greater opportunity now to be accepted into the major leagues with other Americans."[4]

Pop died in 1965. Eight years later, he was inducted into the Baseball Hall of Fame.

Pop Lloyd was known for his easy ways and sense of humor.

Women in the Negro Leagues

Mamie "Peanut" Johnson

Calling Mamie Johnson "Peanut" was fine with her. She understood. At 5-foot-4, she wasn't the biggest or the most fearsome baseball player.

But saying she couldn't play in the women's professional baseball league because she was black? That was a problem.

Instead, Mamie earned a spot in the men's Negro League. She pitched three seasons for the Indianapolis Clowns. One of her teammates was Hank Aaron, MLB's future home-run king. The Clowns signed her in 1953, when she was 19. In her first season, she went 11-3, then went 10-1 and 12-4. She said Hall of Famer Satchel Paige taught her to throw a curveball.

Mamie also played second base and hit between .252 and .284 each season.

As for being rejected by the white women's league (which was showcased in the 1992 movie *A League of Their Own,* starring Tom Hanks, Geena Davis, and Madonna), Mamie found the silver lining. "If I had played with white girls, I would have been just another player, but now I am somebody who has done something that no other woman has done."[5]

After baseball, Mamie became a nurse.

Toni Stone was the first woman to play professionally against men. She joined the Indianapolis Clowns shortly before Mamie in 1953. A second baseman,

Toni Stone

she played just one season, hitting .243 in 50 games. She got a hit off Satchel Paige, and played against future Hall of Famers Willie Mays and Ernie Banks.

Toni left baseball after that season. Like Mamie, she also became a nurse. In 1993, she was inducted into the Women's Sports Hall of Fame in Long Island, New York.

Toni's replacement at second base was Connie Morgan. Batting third in the lineup, she hit around .300. Oscar Charleston, the Clowns manager, called Morgan "one of the most sensational female players" he had ever seen.[6]

Jackie Robinson shares batting tips with Connie Morgan.

1884   Moses "Fleetwood" Walker becomes the first African-American player in Major League Baseball, signing with Toledo of the American Association.

1885   The first all-black professional team, the Cuban Giants, is founded in Babylon, New York.

1887   The National Colored Base Ball League, the first attempt at a professional Negro league, is formed. It includes teams from Pittsburgh, New York, Baltimore, Boston, Cincinnati, Philadelphia, and Louisville.

1890   The International League bans African-American players. The ban lasts until 1946.

1895   Bud Fowler forms the Page Fence Giants, one of black baseball's early powerhouse teams. Based in Adrian, Michigan, the club tours the Midwest and East in its own railroad car. It takes on all comers, including MLB's Cincinnati Reds.

1896   In the *Plessy v. Ferguson* case, the U.S. Supreme Court upholds Louisiana's law requiring "separate but equal" public facilities for blacks. The decision makes race segregation legal throughout the country.

         The Page Fence Giants and the Cuban Giants play a series called a "national championship series." Page Fence wins 10 of the 15 games to earn the championship.

1920   Andrew "Rube" Foster, renowned pitcher and owner of the Chicago American Giants, calls Midwestern team owners to Kansas City. They form the Negro National League. It begins the season on May 2 with the following teams: Chicago American Giants, Chicago Giants, Dayton Marcos, Detroit Stars, Indianapolis ABCs, Kansas City Monarchs, and Cuban Stars. The Negro Southern League begins play in the South. League cities include Atlanta, Nashville, Birmingham, Memphis, New Orleans, and Chattanooga.

1923   Ed Bolden (owner of the Hilldale Club) and Nat Strong (owner of the Brooklyn Royal Giants) organize the Eastern Colored League. The six-team league has Hilldale, Brooklyn, Bacharach Giants, Lincoln Giants, Baltimore Black Sox, and Cuban Stars.

1924   The first Negro World Series is played between the Kansas City Monarchs (Negro National League champs) and the Hilldale Club (Eastern Colored League champs). Kansas City wins the series, 5 games to 4.

1928   The Eastern Colored League folds in midseason. The American Negro League is formed in the East. It has the Homestead Grays, Hilldale Club, Baltimore Black Sox, Lincoln Grays, Bacharach Giants, and Cuban Stars.

1929   The stock market crashes and the Great Depression begins.

1932   The Negro Southern League is the only major black league in operation. It starts the season with only five teams: Indianapolis ABCs, Detroit Stars, Louisville White Sox, Chicago American Giants, and Cleveland Cubs.

1933   A new Negro National League is formed. Organized by Pittsburgh bar owner Gus Green, it starts with seven teams, including the Indianapolis ABCs, the Nashville Elite Giants, and the Louisville Black Caps. Later that year, the first East-West Colored All-Star Game is played at Chicago's Comiskey Park. More than 20,000 fans watched the West beat the East 11-7.

1937   The Negro American League is formed. The seven-team league includes the St. Louis Stars, Kansas City Monarchs, Cincinnati Tigers, and Chicago American Giants.

Home run hitters Josh Gibson and Buck Leonard lead the Homestead Grays to their first of nine straight Negro National League titles.

Joe Louis, a black boxer and national hero, wins the heavyweight championship of the world by knocking out James Braddock, a white boxer.

1946   Jackie Robinson signs with the Brooklyn Dodgers. He starts with a minor league team, the Montreal Royals.

1947   Home run king Josh Gibson dies at age 35.

Jackie Robinson is promoted from the minors to the Brooklyn Dodgers. He is the first black player in Major League Baseball in the modern era. He wins National League rookie of the year. The Dodgers win the National League pennant.

The Cleveland Indians sign Larry Doby, the first black player to play in the American League.

1948   Satchel Paige signs with the Cleveland Indians. At 42, he is the oldest rookie in MLB history. The Negro National League folds at the end of the season.

1952   More than 150 former Negro League players have joined the Major League Baseball system, either in the major or minor leagues. The Negro League era is over.

Chapter 1. Cool Papa Bell

1. William Rogers, "Cool Papa Bell," *Mississippi History Now*, January 2008, http://mshistorynow.mdah.state.ms.us/articles/277/cool-papa-bell

2. "Diamond Lightning: James Thomas 'Cool Papa' Bell," March 7, 2013, http://jkkelley.org/2013/03/07/diamond_lightning-james-thomas-cool-papa-bell/

3. Rogers.

4. Ibid.

Chapter 2 Satchel Paige

1. Satchel Paige Quotes, http://www.satchelpaige.com/quote2.html

2. Official Satchel Paige Site, http://www.satchelpaige.com/

3. Dave Studeman, "Looking Back at Satchel Paige," *Hard Ball Times*, July 2, 2009, http://www.hardballtimes.com/looking-back.

4. Satchel Paige Quotes.

5. Ibid.

Chapter 3. Oscar Charleston

1. Oscar Charleston Biography, http://www.badassoftheweek.com/index.cgi?id=76256892766

2. National Baseball Hall of Fame, "Oscar Charleston," http://baseballhall.org/hof/charleston-oscar

3. "Oscar Charleston," Baseball Reference.com, February 2, 2016, http://www.baseball-reference.com/bullpen/Oscar_Charleston

4. National Baseball Hall of Fame.

5. Ken Mandel, "Five-tool Player: Charleston Considered Best All-Around Player in Negro Leagues," *Negro Leagues Legacy*, MLB.com, http://mlb.mlb.com/mlb/history/mlb_negro_leagues_profile.jsp?player=charleston_oscar

6. Frazier Robinson, with Paul Bauer, *Catching Dreams: My Life in the Negro Baseball Leagues* (Syracuse: Syracuse University Press, 1999), p. 144.

Chapter 4. Josh Gibson

1 Tom Singer, "Powerful Bat: Gibson the Best Home Run Hitter in Negro Leagues," *Negro Leagues Legacy*, MLB.com http://mlb.mlb.com/mlb/history/mlb_negro_leagues_profile.jsp?player=gibson_josh

2. Larry Schwart, "No Joshing about Gibson's Talents," ESPN.com, n.d. https://espn.go.com/sportscentury/features/00016050.html

3 Josh Gibson Historical Marker, http://explorepahistory.com/hmarker.php?markerId=1-A-13

Chapter 5. John "Pop" Lloyd

1. "John Henry 'Pop' Lloyd," National Baseball Hall of Fame and Museum, http://baseballhall.org/hof/lloyd-pop

2. "John Henry 'Pop' Lloyd," Negro Leagues Baseball Museum, http://coe.k-state.edu/annex/nlbemuseum/history/players/lloydjh.html

3. Ibid.

4. Ibid.

5. "Mamie 'Peanut' Johnson, a Strong Right Arm," *African American Registry*, http://www.aaregistry.org/historic_events/view/mamie-peanut-johnson-strong-right-arm

6. Martha Ackmann, *Curveball: The Remarkable Story of Toni Stone, the First Woman to Play Professional Baseball in the Negro League* (Chicago: Lawrence Hill Books, 2010), p. 204.

Works Consulted

Baseball Reference.com. http://www.baseball-reference.com

"The Black Woman of Pro Baseball: Toni Stone." African American Registry. http://www.aaregistry.org/historic_events/viewblack-woman-pro-baseball-toni-stone

"Diamond Lightning: James Thomas 'Cool Papa' Bell," March 7, 2013, http://jkkelley.org/2013/03/07/diamond_lightning-james-thomas-cool-papa-bell/

Josh Gibson Historical Marker. http://explorepahistory.com/hmarker.php?markerId=1-A-13

Major League Baseball: Negro Leagues Legacy. http://mlb.mlb.com/mlb/history/mlb_negro_leagues.jsp

"Mamie 'Peanut' Johnson, a Strong Right Arm." *African American Registry*. http://www.aaregistry.org/historic_events/view/mamie-peanut-johnson-strong-right-arm

"Mamie 'Peanut' Johnson, Pitching Pioneer." NPR, November 30, 2009. http://www.npr.org/templates/story/story.php?storyId=1164167

National Baseball Hall of Fame and Museum. http://baseballhall.org

Negro Baseball League. http://www.negroleaguebaseball.com/

Negro League Baseball. http://www.negroleaguebaseball.com

Negro Leagues Baseball Museum. http://coe.k-state.edu/annex/nlbemuseum/nlbemuseum.html

Oscar Charleston bio. http://www.badassoftheweek.com/index.cgi?id=76256892766

Richards, Phil. "Retro Indy: Oscar Charleston." *Indianapolis Star,* October 14, 2014. http://www.indystar.com/story/news/history/retroindy/2014/10/14/oscar-charleston/17252007/

Rogers, William. "Cool Papa Bell," *Mississippi History Now*, January 2008, http://mshistorynow.mdah.state.ms.us/articles/277/cool-papa-bell

"Satchel Paige: Unsung Hero." NPR, July 29, 2009. http://www.npr.org/templates/story/story.php?storyId=111063901

Satchel Paige Official Site. http://www.satchelpaige.com/

Schwart, Larry. "No Joshing about Gibson's Talents," ESPN.com, n.d. https://espn.go.com/sportscentury/features/00016050.html

Studeman, Dave. "Looking Back at Satchel Paige." *The Hard Ball Times,* July 2, 2009. http://www.hardballtimes.com/looking-back.

Thomas, Robert. "Toni Stone, 75, First Woman to Play Big-League Baseball." *The New York Times*, November 10, 1996. http://www.nytimes.com/1996/11/10/sports/toni-stone-75-first-woman-to-play-big-league-baseball.html

Tye, Larry. "Satchel Paige: Confronting Racism One Fastball at a Time." NPR, July 17, 2011. http://www.npr.org/templates/story/story.php?storyId=105037269

Tye, Larry. *Satchel: The Life and Times of an American Legend.* New York: Random House, 2009.

Books

Cieradkowski, Gary. *The League of Outsider Baseball: An Illustrated History of Baseball's Forgotten Heroes.* New York: Touchstone, 2015.

Gorman, Carol. *Stumptown Kid.* (Fiction.) Atlanta: Peachtree Publishers, 2015.

Klima, John. *Willie's Boys: The 1948 Birmingham Black Barons, The Last Negro League World Series, and the Making of a Baseball Legend.* Hoboken, N.J.: John Wiley & Son. , 2009.

Took, Wes. *King of the Mound: My Summer with Satchel Paige.* (Fiction.) New York: Simon & Schuster, 2013.

On the Internet

Castrovince, Anthony. "Teen's Research Brings Negro Leagues to Life." MLB.com, February 7, 2012. http://m.mlb.com/news/article/26592208/

Fun Trivia: The Negro Leagues http://www.funtrivia.com/en/Sports/Negro-Leagues-15001.html

Negro League History 101. http://www.negroleaguebaseball.com/history101.html

Neubauer, Riley. "Negro Leagues Baseball Museum: An In-Depth Look at Baseball's Past." *SI For Kids,* November 25, 2015. http://www.sikids.com/si-kids/2016/01/12/trip-negro-leagues-baseball-museum

Baseball Hall of Fame (BAYSS-bawl HAWL uv FAYM)—A museum in Cooperstown, New York, that honors great baseball players, coaches, umpires, and other officials.

bigotry (BIG-uh-tree)—Hating or refusing to accept the members of a particular group.

commissioner (kuh-MIH-shuh-ner)—The person in charge of an organization.

corporal (KOR-prul)—In the army, an officer that ranks above an army private first class and below a sergeant.

curveball (KURV-ball)—A pitch that appears to drop or curve as it nears home plate.

exhibition (ek-suh-BIH-shun)—A game or series that does not count in the official standings or is not part of official league play.

home run (home RUHN)—In baseball, a hit that allows a runner to circle all four bases and score.

Hoosier (HOO-zyur)—The official name for anyone from the state of Indiana.

inning (IN-ing)—One of usually nine periods in baseball in which each team bats. The team at bat tries to score before getting three outs.

Major League Baseball (MAY-jur LEEG BAYSS-bawl)—The top professional baseball league in the United States.

manager (MAN-uh-jur)—The person who directs or has control of an organization such as a baseball team.

Negro Leagues (NEE-groh LEEGZ)—The professional leagues for mostly African American players who were not allowed to play in the all-white leagues.

prejudice (PREH-joo-dis)—Angry feelings about people based on the color of their skin, their religion, or where they are from.

racism (RAY-sism)—A belief that people who look or act like oneself are better than others, and that it is okay to be mean to those others.

sandlot ball (sand-LOT BAWL)—A game played on an empty lot instead of on an official field.

semipro (SEH-mee-proh)—Short for *semiprofessional* (seh-mee-proh-FEH-shuh-nul). Playing for a small amount of money, but not enough to make a living.

sharecropper (SHAYR-krop-er)—A farmer who earns part of the crops that are grown on someone else's land.

spikes (SPIKES)—Sharp pieces sticking out of the bottom of shoes to make it easier to run.

strikeout (STRIKE out)—In baseball, when a pitcher gets three strikes on a hitter without the hitter putting the ball in play.

stroke (STROHK)—A sometimes fatal condition in which a blood vessel in the brain bursts, causing brain damage.

PHOTO CREDITS: P.9—Paul Sableman; p. 11—Maggie Cordova; p. 15—Sevarini; p. 25—Pulp International; p. 33—Verdun2. All other photos—Public Domain. Every measure has been taken to find all copyright holders of material used in this book. In the event any mistakes or omissions have happened within, attempts to correct them will be made in future editions of the book.